more than a friend
Love
Marie I Ball

HOPE

Thats All There Is

Marie I. Ball

authorHOUSE®

AuthorHouse™
1663 Liberty Drive, Suite 200
Bloomington, IN 47403
www.authorhouse.com
Phone: 1-800-839-8640

First published by AuthorHouse 8/7/2007

ISBN: 978-1-4343-1900-5 (sc)

Library of Congress Control Number: 2007904658

Printed in the United States of America
Bloomington, Indiana

This book is printed on acid-free paper.

FORWORD

From the beginning of time, wars and rumors of war were the norm. What we forget is the result, refugees. The less fortunate people who can do nothing but try to find some place to call home even for a while, must move, move, move. Some find peace in death while others suffer the pangs of hunger, disease, and degradation. When I first heard a story about this family, I could not believe it. After delving into history, I have found hundreds of stories to match it. The lost lives of so many have weighed heavily on me, I offer this as a hope for all refugees.

1902

We were a small family living in our beloved Armenia. We had two lovely young girls, the oldest, Nofina, was age fourteen, and Semuramis was twelve—we call her Siny. I was a shopkeeper; my wife stayed home to care for us.

Our living was beginning to be a little complicated by Turks who were becoming more and more aggressive. Turkey surrounds us on three sides, but they came from the north, where the sultan ruled with an iron hand. They lived, we were told, the life we could not understand. They had rich food, fruit, and meat the likes of which no one in Armenia had ever seen. They dressed in gold and silver and silk from the Orient. They took anything and anybody they wanted. The proof of this was the harems full of young girls.

"Hide! Hide! Run! Run! The Turks! The Turks!"

They came shouting with turbans flying and horses gleaming in the sun; they laughed like children.

It was a wild scene of horses stomping into homes and stepping on people. Ataturk, son of the sultan, grunted and looked around the house. Ataturk was a tall, young, bronzed man of about twenty. He looked at me and said, "Nofina." My God! He wanted my fourteen-year-old daughter! I acted as if I didn't know what he meant, and he finally left. It was well known that they would take girls, and maybe you'd see them again, and maybe not.

We stayed one more day, and then my wife Marig and I decided we had better leave, or our girls would be lost to the Turks. We gathered our few belongings and slipped out after dark. We would make our way to the Black Sea, staying in Armenia for as long as possible.

On the first night, we slept in a church. Most of Armenia

was Christian, so the churches were open at all times. That night passed uneventfully, as did the second night. We were beginning to think that maybe we had made a mistake.

We decided to travel during the day until we reached the town of Mardin. There we met another family who were fleeing also. The Turks had taken their home. They were trying to get to Bulgaria. We thought that together we could help one another. That night, while sleeping, we were startled by horses pounding in the streets. We were told to go up to the church tower. There we stayed, listening to the noise as well as the screams of people. We dared not look down for fear that someone would see us. But the cries! Oh! The screams of agony and pain were such you could never forget.

At dawn they rode off to the countryside, and we could hear them making camp; they were still yelling and laughing. In town, the people were confused, hurt, and bewildered, but they were trying to help the wounded and bury the dead. It was a terrible sight. Helping was necessary, but we could do very little. The Turks had made no distinction between men, women, and children. What did they want? Was it just fun? Was Ataturk just a monster? It is hard to try to understand.

We slept in the church tower that night, but Ataturk and his men were gone by the late morning. We stayed to help, but we felt we were on borrowed time. On the third day, it was as if I could sense Ataturk getting closer, so we left. There were now eight of us, but more people were getting ready to leave. We hoped to get to the mountains where some of our family had made homes. The Turks had never invaded the mountains, so we felt we would be safe there.

Our trip was uneventful as we traveled by day or night whenever we felt. Others did too, so because people were on the road all the time, we felt safer. If a place seemed calm and peaceful, we would stay a few more days and try to find work.

We had no more news about raids or any men on horseback, so we all decided to stay here for a while before we headed into the mountains. We rested, still in our beloved Armenia. We were like a little village. We made camp; we cooked; we played. We had not been this happy for a long time. We prayed and we sang. It was a good feeling. Maybe it was all over and we could go home.

Hopes are so very deceiving. It was not long after this that we received news that more villages were being attacked. The Turks were getting braver and braver. The Kurds were beginning to attack towns as well. Where did they come from? They were coming from all sides. I picked up two rocks from Armenia to take with us to the mountains. I would hold them in my hands to remind me of home. So we resumed our trip into the mountains. We were very tired of running. My family welcomed us with open arms. It was wonderful to be there. They had a nice house, a garden, and a cart. They fed us and let us sleep as long as we wanted, and we talked about old times in Moush.

People were leaving Armenia in bunches, so every day news came to us. To our surprise, there were rumors that Ataturk was invading the mountains! My family took us to a big cave that was high up in the mountains and told us to hide there. We were there three days. It wasn't so bad. Then my family appeared again. Ataturk was in town looking for Nofina! What a shock! We all stayed in the cave hoping he would go away. Then we heard the rumble of horses on the mountain. We went deep into the cave—further and further inside. It was dark and damp, and only fear kept us going. All of a sudden, we turned a corner, and there was light with a waterfall, and the rocks seemed to glow. We fell on our knees and thanked God. Little did we know we would be here for over a month.

Ataturk and his men made camp in the front part of the

cave. There was constant loud talking, yelling, and singing. They would leave in the morning and come back late in the afternoon. It seemed they stayed forever, and then they were gone. We hid for another two or three days, but when they didn't come back, we left too. My cousin went back to her home, and we crossed over the mountain to Persia.

In Persia, we found work and decided to stay. They gave us a little house where we could eat and sleep. Marig and the girls worked in the field, and I worked with the sheep. I was content to stay, but after a while, Marig was anxious to leave. The word from Armenia was not good, and more and more people were coming over the mountains and into Persia. It was not good. Bad signs were everywhere, and there were more stories of raids and killings. Our friends Ruds and Arax and their families had not stopped as we had. They moved on to Bulgaria. We had been on the run for four years. We were very tired, and the girls were very tired of running. Nerves were very frayed.

It was 1906, and Persia was having problems too. We moved on. Some countries were not friendly. This time we did not stop until we were in Bulgaria. There were lots of Armenians here, but they were not welcome. It was noisy and dirty, and no one wanted us there, so on we went, moving toward the Mediterranean Sea. Why I don't know. We prayed to find some place where we could be safe.

One day we came to the Sea of Marmara. We were on the Turkish side of the water, but the mountains were very high, so we felt there was not much danger. We were traveling mostly by night and trying to hide during the day . We were now being very quiet. (Lots of people were on the road.) We were dirty, and our clothes were in shreds. Nofina was in a bad mood. She'd been scared, hungry, and cold for so long that she decided to go into the water and clean herself. The girls both got in and were just sitting there. It was very refreshing. Marig and I decided to do the same. Before we knew it, lots of others got in too. It was an eerie sight—people in the water being very quiet but smiling to themselves. Nofina was in her outer clothes, as was Simy. They were a lovely sight to behold when they were all wet. As we slowly got out, I noticed some people moving about who had not been in the water. I had always told my girls that if any man came toward them, they should put dirt on their faces and pull their *charshaff* close to their heads. I sidled up to the girls and whispered, "Danger!" The girls quickly put their *charshaff* on and picked up sand from the water. When a man put his hand on Nofina, instead of putting the sand or dirt on her face, she slapped his hand. There was a rock in her hand, so when she hit him, it cut the flesh. He let out a scream and ran. We quickly gathered up our things, and wet as we were, we started walking again.

Around dawn, we found another cave to sleep in. We were not the only ones there, but we were all trying to rest. At dusk, we were ready again, and down the hill we started walking. We reached the road and found bodies everywhere.

The men on horseback had been there.

Now we traveled by night and hid in the hills and trees during the day. We reached the town of Imbros on the Aegean Sea. There we could get a boat to Greece. We were very excited. At last we could rest for a while—if we could get on the boat. Dozens of people were doing the same. Most captains wanted only people who had lots of money. Then, if they had any room left, they'd take the refugees and squeeze as much money out of them as they could. It took us a few days to find a ride, but we finally did. It was a small boat, and it was dirty. The captain was dirty too. But we could get on! We were on that boat for two days. We lived in a cabin in the bowels of the boat with eight other people. It was stifling; there was no room to sit down. It was awful, but we'd survived thus far, and we would survive this too.

In Greece it wasn't so bad. People tried to help us. Now the world was beginning to know about the Turks and the

Kurds. We found a shop owner who would let us stay in his back room if I worked for him. Marig and the girls helped out too by cleaning the shop. It wasn't bad, but paid little. We rested, we ate, and we slept. I was content, but Marig was very nervous. When a customer told her he was going to America, Marig was insistent that we find a way to go too. I wanted to stay here and see Greece. It was different from anywhere we had been. The people even dressed differently. The girls liked it here too. Marig won. We would try to go to America. That meant that we would have to find a way to get to the Mediterranean Sea, find a boat that would go to America, and pay to go.

The shop owner, Mr. Peter Allan, was very helpful. He knew people who could get us to the coast, and then we'd be on our own. He arranged for us to go in a truck. We would be sitting in the back with boxes of tobacco. We had accumulated some things, especially the girls. Mr. Allan had given us two boxes which were not too big, for we had to carry them, but to where we didn't know. It was a long trip in Greece. Riding was good, but it didn't last long enough. People were nice to us but wary of us, so we just kept moving. Sometimes we'd find a barn and we'd sleep on hay. (To this day, I love the smell of hay.) Prennser was the town we landed in on the Mediterranean Sea. We walked along the beach until we came to a stretch with a few people on it. We sat down, and for the first time since we left our hometown, we felt safe. We sat there and cried and cried and cried. We had made it.

It was great, but soon it was time to try to find a boat to take us to America. The urgency in our lives made it hard to rest or relax; it was very difficult even to live. On the beach, several people were just resting or swimming but not talking to one another. We kept to ourselves and talked in lowered voices. A group came by us, and one man started toward us. My heart was in my mouth. Then he smiled, and in a halting voice, speaking Armenian (very badly), asked us if we were the family from the shop in Greece. It was the young man who had told us about going to America! He told us the group he was with was going to America too. So, if we wanted to follow them, we could. (I noticed he was sneaking looks at Nofina, and she was looking at him.) For the first time in a long time, the girls started combing their hair and primping. It made me smile, but Marig did not like it.

The ship didn't seem to be large enough to go to America, but we got on. To our amazement, it was only a few hours later that we had to get off and get on a larger ship. It was so big it scared me. And the people! There were lots and lots of them. Some were all dressed up with a lot of luggage, but most were like us—carrying boxes that held all their earthly possession. For the first time, I thought about how we must look. We were four very tired, bedraggled people with our two boxes. The well-dressed people were taken aboard the ship first, and then people like us were directed to the lower rooms. The rooms were sparse, with only two beds. But it looked like heaven to us since only our small family would be living in it. The joy we felt could not be described. We would look at each other and cry and laugh and hug one another. We had a room of our own for a while. It was wonderful!

People were roaming around the ship, but Marig wanted us to stay in our room. She was very cautious about the people; she didn't trust anyone. About the third day out, she let the girls go out and look around. It was very interesting to see so many people just like us. We met some who were also from Armenia. They were friendly, but very wary. We ate our cheese and bread. When we found the bathtub, our girls were truly in heaven!

About the fourth day, we were beginning to feel at home. Marig insisted that either she or I should go with the girls when they left the room. Nofina was eighteen by now, and Simy was sixteen. They were both striking girls—a little on the skinny side, but with long, dark hair and lovely brown eyes.

As with any children their age, they were looking for what comes next. Marig was terrified for them both, insisting they wear their *charshaff* at all times when they left the room.

By the fifth day, we all roamed about the ship comfortably. We met many people: the stranger named Abdiel, Rudy and Arax, and even my own cousin, Sarkis, and his family.

They had been driven out of their homes by the Turks also. We were all going to America to start new lives. Sarkie and his wife stayed close to us, and we talked about what we would do. We finally decided to try to find work to enable us to live close to one another. Sadly, this did not happen. We were lucky to find jobs and a place to live. They went to New Jersey to work.

We were on that boat for fifteen days, and on the fourteenth day, Adbiel came to our room and handed me a piece of paper. He also told me to give it to the authorities if we had any problems when we left the ship. I tried to read it, but all I could make out was "…a job was waiting for us…"

We docked on a beautiful day in September. All around us people were smiling and laughing as they met the familiar faces of people they knew. We were nervous, yet excited, as we did not know what lay ahead for us.

The well-dressed people with all their luggage were in line with people like us who were still carrying their boxes of precious possession. No difference was shown, and when it was our turn, they searched our two boxes and I showed them our paper and that was it! We were in America! Our hearts were racing; everything was so exciting and different from anything we'd ever known or seen. We walked around gazing at all the people and hurrying through the streets. When we saw a policeman, I panicked, but he just grunted. I showed him our paper and he directed us to a shop. It was a dress shop. As we walked in, the woman in charge looked us over, smiled, and told us where we could find a place to live. We found the boarding house and were given two rooms—one for Marig and me and one for the two girls. Two meals were included, and what a scene it was when we sat down to eat! There were twelve people crowded around a table that was covered with more food than I had ever seen at one meal. There were pork chops, potatoes, ham, vegetables, and fresh fruit. We had existed by eating only bread and cheese for so long that it was hard to take in. We couldn't eat much, and Marig and the girls were sick afterward.

The first day at the shop went quite well. The customers would pick out pictures or tell Sara (the owner) what she wanted, then Sara would measure them, make patterns, and cut them out. Marig's job would be to sew them together. But today she watched and absorbed it all as the pieces were transformed into the desired garments. I found the whole process quite fascinating. Knowing Marig and the girls would be safe in the shop all day, I went looking for work. I found it, too, in a tobacco shop. The shopkeeper was a tough old man who expected me to work, work, work. I was grateful for the job, and I looked forward to going every day. It was absolute relief to not have to be afraid every minute of every day.

We all settled into our daily routines more easily than I had expected. Marig and the girls were learning a lot, and they all loved sewing the beautiful dresses. Marig would collect all our money on payday. First to be paid was our room and board, and then we'd save every penny that wasn't needed for personal items. We had a goal: a home of our own in America!

The shopkeeper kept me very busy all day long, but I didn't mind. I was in America! Each day seemed to just fly by. Marig and the girls were just as busy, but they didn't mind either. One day, Abdiel appeared at their shop. Sara seemed quite flustered, and she bowed and smiled at him as he talked quietly to her. It seemed she couldn't do enough for him. She gave him coffee and cake as he sat and watched her proudly display her completed garments. He was definitely a valued customer. He managed to catch Nofina's eye and wink at her. She was totally caught off guard, and she turned bright red with embarrassment. As he was leaving the shop, he quietly walked over to her and whispered, "I'll pick you up at seven." Nofina didn't know whether to believe him or not. She really thought he was kidding, but did allow herself to think how nice it would be!

At seven o'clock, Nofina was still dressed for work, and Marig was more than curious as to why she refused to eat and continually combed her hair. Mai, our landlord, came upstairs and knocked on our door to tell us a Mr. Abdiel was calling on us. We all scurried down to the parlor, and there he was, looking very much the gentleman. He greeted us warmly and asked if the girls could go out for a while. I could see the disappointment on Nofina's face when he said *girls*. Apprehension was all over Marig's face, but she said nothing. I agreed, but allowed them to go with Abdiel. They arrived home a few hours later, filled with excitement and chatter about where they had been and what they had seen. They had actually been to a real restaurant and strolled around window shopping in the numerous shops. They had even seen their first movie theatre and had arrived back home in a taxi!

After that night, Abdiel developed the habit of stopping at the shop, winking at Nofina, and then coming by the house that evening. Each adventure took them further and further from the boarding house until they saw the real theatres. People were all dressed in long white gloves, diamonds, furs, and gorgeous dresses. Each time, they'd nearly explode through the door, filled with excitement and the details of everything they'd seen and experienced. Then Abdiel was gone. Weeks and then a month went by, and he didn't appear. Just as abruptly, he reappeared with no explanation for his absence.

One day in 1909, Marig came home white as a sheet, all

upset, and carrying a newspaper in her hand. We read the terrible news of 230,000 Armenians having been massacred by the Turks and the Kurds. We were all terrified once again. Marig took a map of the United States from her pocket, opened it, and pointed to a city in the middle of the country-St. Louis, Missouri. That's where we would go. We would tell no one. We'd even change our names. She was shaking with fright. So Marig became Mary; Nofina became Athena; Simy became Lizabeth, or Liz; I became Michael; and we took the surname of Mr. Allen. So we became Mary Allen, Lizabeth Allen, Athena Allen, and Michael Allen. I was afraid we were moving too quickly, but Marig was terrified, and we had always listened to her, and she seemed always to be right.

We made plans to go in one week. The girls did not want to go, and Nofina wanted to leave a message for Abdiel, but her mother said no. Oh, and one more thing: we would not speak Armenian, only English, and we would all study to become citizens.

Once we had made the decision to do all this, Marig seemed to calm down. At the shop, Nofina talked to Sara and tried to find out a few things about Abdiel, but all she would say was that he bought clothes for his mother and sisters.

We left in the night, just as we had when we left our home in Armenia. This time we each had a box. On the train we found two facing seats and we four sat down, exhausted by the tension and strain of the last week. As the train started to move, we all seemed to relax. It was different than when we left Moush. The train was not crowded, so when they dimmed the lights, we all fell asleep.

We awoke to a countryside that was very beautiful. There were green fields and animals, and when there were people, they would wave. It was very—*peaceful* was the word. The first stop we made was in a little town, and we were told we'd be there for two hours. We got off to stretch our legs.

People would pass us, tip their hats, and smile. There was no hurrying here. Once back on the train, we just sat and looked out of the windows. It was a wonder. The fields were very green. Cattle were everywhere—big herds that were very fat and healthy. Sometimes you'd see a man on horseback gently riding by the herd and then moving slowly toward a water hole or to greener pasture. Compared to our other travels, this seemed very different. There was no hurrying; no animosity. Everyone seemed very peaceful. The land seemed to stretch on forever.

At the next stop, we were told we'd be there for quite a while and that there was a place to eat in town. We walked up one side of the town. There was a saloon and a store that was interesting, as it had all kinds of food and also fabric that was very beautiful. Marig and the girls just had to have some. They picked pink fabric with little flowers on it. They hoped that dresses could later be made for them out of it. On the other side of the street, was a man shoeing horses, which was very interesting, and there was a little store that had a single seamstress. We went in, and a very nice lady told us pretty much the same thing that Sara had told us about how she made dresses. We bid the lady good day, and next door was the place to eat. Some passengers from the train were already there. We ordered and found the food quite good. Mary seemed to tire about then, so we went back to the train. As we pulled out of the station, we were full of not only food, but also of much satisfaction for the fine life, the wonderful country, and the great free people. Our hearts were full—very full—of happiness.

The last stop we made was to change trains. We were only there about an hour, but we did buy a paper. We read it together and smiled. McDonald's cow had jumped the fence and eaten Mr. Smith's garden. The news sounded good. Mary was not feeling well, and I was getting concerned, so when we returned to the train, I took another seat, and she lay down.

The porter came through shouting, "St Louis! St. Louis!" We were so tired we could not get excited. We gathered our boxes, and when we left the train, it seemed like we finally were home. As we exited the station at three thirty in the afternoon, it seemed there was a little busyness going on. Guess we were near a business section. We walked down the street, and there was a little house with a "For Rent" sign. Mary was looking and muttering to herself. (We could not be so lucky as to find a place such as this to rent.) A young woman came out of the house next door and smiled at us. "My mother died, so I am renting her house," she said. "It has two bedrooms, a living room, a kitchen and one bathroom." Before we could say a word, Mary asked, "Can we see it?" Inside was furniture and things, as if someone had just moved out. The lady (Mrs. Donahue) said we could use her mother's things if we wanted. Almost like a dream, we went in and it felt like it belonged to us. It was our home now.

We rested for a few days, and when we decided to look for work, Mary made her announcement. "I will not be going to work this time. I am with child." We all were very excited. A baby—how grand! That's all we could think about—a little baby!

The first shop the girls went to hired them. It was a small place, but very busy. I found a job close to them in a tobacco shop. Things were okay. I would walk down to their shop and we'd walk home together.

Life was good. A routine always makes for contentment. At home, Mary was cleaning,

cooking (Armenian style), and having a great time with her house. One night, exactly three months later, we were eating our evening meal when someone knocked on our door. I went to the door, and to our surprise it was Abdiel! "How? How did you find us?" I said. He just smiled and came into the kitchen and sat down. Athena was almost jumping because she was so pleased. He was looking at her with a great deal of love in his eyes. No one could mistake his feelings or thoughts. He first told us he had found the map with a pencil mark on St. Louis, and that gave him a clue.

Then he had a big story to tell us. Here is his story:

"My mother and I were captured by the sultan when I was very young. When I was eight years old, my mother persuaded the sultan to send me to boarding school in America. As I grew older, I would visit my mother in the harem, and I loved all the women. So I would bring presents for them. I remained in America doing business, but always found dresses for my mother and the other women. My stepbrother, Ataturk, had told me to catch Nofina, for he thought he loved her. But after a few years, he grew tired of 'Catch Nofina.' But by this time, I had become too fond of Nofina. I did not realize how fond until you left and I thought I would never see you again."

When he told the story, we were all so terrified at first that we didn't know what to think. He said he was going to visit his mother, and then he would be back to see us. After he left, Athena had nightmares about the deaths, the murders, and the horror of our past. How could she reconcile all of that, even for love? For days after, when I would walk home with Liz and Athena, she would talk and talk, trying to figure it out. Then one day as we reached home, we could hear voices laughing and talking in Armenian. That was unusual, for we did not speak Armenian. As we reached the door, we saw a woman with Mary and Abdiel. It was Abdiel's mother, and she told us that she was Armenian and that she was not going back to Turkey.

Abdiel and Athena went out the front door, and as I saw them embrace and kiss, I knew they would work everything out.

Abdiel found a nice place to live with his mother, and so they (he and Athena) began to plan their wedding. It was a joyous time. Mari made Liz a dress from the pink fabric with little flowers, and Athena's dress was to be made from material Anna had brought with her. Mary was very happy, and almost every day, Anna came to visit and help with the dresses, and they talked continually about the wedding, the baby, and Armenia. It was perfect. We all were very happy.

Abdiel had to go out of town on business, so we tried to get Anna to stay with us, but no, she would stay by herself. Abdiel came home on Thursday. He hugged Athena and then asked where his mother was. We were surprised, for we had not seen her since Abdiel's last visit. He really began to worry. I went with him back to the house where he lived, and we searched very carefully, looking for Anna or clues. One thing we found was that Anna's jewels were missing. The gown she wore in the harem was gone, but her other Western clothes were still hanging in her closet. Abdiel sat on the bed and put his hands over his face. "I know Ataturk was here." His father, the sultan, wanted my mother not because he loved her, but because he wanted to show her she belonged to him. What to do! What to do! We returned to my house to talk more about what we should do. Abdiel decided he would go back to Turkey and try to rescue his

mother. That night, Mary and I talked until the wee hours of

the morning. I would go with Abdiel. He was very pleased

about the dangers, but concerned about what could happen.

I would not be deterred. It was decided we would dress as

reformed Turks (long black coats buttoned up to the chin

and loose trousers, but wearing a turban). Abdiel felt we

would not be noticed if we were dressed like this because

most reformed Turks were lower on the economic scale. We

had a room on the train, and we ate in the dining car. I

learned a lot about him on this trip. He was a man who was

looking for answers. Why had the Turks taken his mother?

Why could he not be in Armenia? He could not remember

Armenia as he so wanted to. The trip was easier this time.

It seemed that doors opened for Abdiel. We traveled with

ease, as only the wealthy can. The boat was another story. We

dressed as the reformed Turks, and people were not so nice to

us. As the boat reached Turkey, Abdiel found horses, and so

our real trip began. We would ride for a while and then stop, and if we saw no one, we would talk about what we would do when we reached the sultan's palace. There were lots of soldiers on the road, but not too many people walking. We rode at the foot of the mountains inside Turkey till we came to a trail that led through the mountains. As we reached the road on the outer side, I realized we were beside the Sea of Marmara. It was very odd to see under these circumstances. There was no rush of people running for their lives. I was thinking of and revisiting the trip I made eleven years ago with my wife and two girls that was very different. Abdiel suddenly stopped. After getting off his horse, he went into the underbrush. I could not imagine why. When I caught up with him, he said, "It's here someplace."

"What?" I asked.

As he pulled the brush away, a cave was uncovered. It wasn't a very big entrance, but we pulled the horses in, walking them slowly till we made torches and lit them.

"You'll see," he said as we walked farther into the cave. It was dirty with webs and bats and so on, as most caves are. Then we came to a wall. It was the end of the cave, or so it seemed. The horses started to snort and fidget. I was afraid they could feel something we couldn't. Abdiel found a spot along the, wall and he and his horse shimmied through. I followed. It was remarkable what we found. There was a long hall that was wide enough to accommodate both of us side by side. At the end was what almost appeared to be a barn for the horses with hay and water.

"How!"

"Ataturk!"

"Who?"

Abdiel spoke very quietly. "One time Ataturk told me about this, but he later said he made it up. I often wondered if it was true. This is how someone confronted Athena that night when she wounded him. They came back, got their horse, and the men attacked the refugees."

As we walked up the stairs from the "barn," it was dark

and scary, and it was very narrow, so I walked first and Abdiel followed. We were being as quiet as we could. The palace sat flush against the mountain, so the stairs were very steep. As we reached the top, we found halls on either side. Abdiel whispered go to the right, and as we rounded a corner, we could hear lots of talking. It was coming from guards—big guys—who were sitting at a table and eating. We quickly turned around to explore the left side. There we came to an abrupt end. There was what looked like a doorway, but there was no way to open it. As we stood there wondering what to do, we heard voices. It was the sultan speaking. We waited in the dark for a long time, not daring to move or speak. The voices went on and on. Abdiel finally whispered, "Let's try the other side again." We turned around and silently walked back to the room where we had heard and seen the guards. As we rounded the corner, no one was in the room, so we ventured in slowly, hardly breathing. It was a horrible-looking place. On one side were cells, and on the other wall hung chains and what looked like a forge without a fire in it. A few people in the cells looked up but said nothing. As we walked down the hall, each confined person looked up, but still no one said a word. As we reached the door, we hesitated for fear a guard was outside. No one was outside in the hall. It was a large open space with lots of closed doors. It was so quiet that it was weird. Abdiel said he had never been here before, so he was thinking about which way and where we should go. After a few minutes, he pointed to the left, and there the stairs sort of curved around and up. We went through a door, and there were statues of marble all along the hallway. It took our breath away. I had never seen anything like it. I guess *impressive* was the word. We looked back into the center of the hall where the room should have been when we heard the voice of the sultan, but the only things in the room were three statues of armor. Then we heard what seemed to be marching soldiers, so we opened the first door we saw on the left side of the hall and went in as quietly as possible. It was full of women. It was the harem. The women just looked up, and when Abdiel took off his turban, they recognized him and very excitedly hugged him and tried to talk to him. Things were changing. They said the sultan had been sent a notice saying there would be only a central government and no sultans anymore. Most of the army had left, and things were very upset. What would they do? Where would they go? The women were near panic. We asked about Anna and they told us she was locked in a room by the sultan's office. They gave us directions, so we quietly opened the door to go, but the hall was full of soldiers from the central government. We rushed back to the women and they surrounded us, and when the soldiers came in, they just nodded and smiled. (The women were very beautiful and dressed very scantily.) The soldiers looked about the room, which was large and had beautiful couches and large pillows in colors I had never seen before. The women were great at hiding us, and they smelled very good. They sort of surrounded us, and with great effort, kept the soldiers from seeing us. They had piled pillows around us and were reclining on the pillows. No one asked them to move. What a relief! I had been holding my breath, so I was exhausted when they finally were gone. Who were they looking for? We didn't understand. We decided to spend the night in the harem quarters. It was amazing. First we had dinner. They put a table on the floor with the food in the center, and we ate while talking and laughing with one another. It was quite pleasant. Then they each got a large pillow and curled up on it and fell asleep. We did the same, but after everyone was sleeping, we decided it was a good time to try and find Anna. We found the sultan's office, but the room Anna was in was locked. We looked for keys everywhere, and then someone opened the door. It was the sultan. At first he was very indifferent, but then he suddenly sat down and put his head in his hands and told us he was to be sent out of the country with only a small amount of money. The soldiers were trying to find him now. Then he made us a deal. If we would help him escape with the women, he would let Anna go with us. One more thing—his son Ataturk would go with us. First we wanted to see Anna. She was fine, but when we told her of the sultan's offer, she was hesitant. "You can't trust him," she said. "He's ruthless and mean." Our time was running out. We had to decide and make a plan now. The soldiers were marching into the palace. Suddenly, the sultan got up and ran into the harem to get the eight women to come with him. As we hurried into the hall, the sultan went toward the three statues of armor. Ataturk was standing there amid a pile of gunpowder. They opened a door to the secret room, and Abdiel, Anna, and I ran in. The women were just behind us then. As Ataturk opened the door (the switch was behind the middle statue of armor), a group of soldiers rushed toward the sultan. In the confusion, the women rushed back to the sultan, so as Ataturk lit the gunpowder, he ran into the room, but the sultan, the women, and the soldiers were caught in the explosion. We tried to get out of the room, but the door would not open; the explosion had jammed it closed. Outside we could hear soldiers running, and then we heard another explosion. The soldiers were running out of the palace. We sat in total darkness for a long time, and then Ataturk lit a lamp. The room was filled with gold and jewels.

The sultan had been storing all his valuables. We didn't know what to say! Ataturk wanted to see if his father was alive, so he insisted I go with him through the inside door, through the dungeon, and into the hall. Everyone there was dead, and the palace was dangerous to be in. As we came back to the secret room, Ataturk told us to find valuables we could hide on our persons. We were dressed in our reformed Turk uniforms, so it was easy to hide things. But for Ataturk, who was in a solider's uniform, it was hard to hide anything. Anna had on a long, gray dress with a white kerchief on her head that she had pulled down to hide her face. Her hair was piled high on her head; she could hide lots of jewels. We decided to leave the room and go down the back stairs. As we did, we heard one more explosion, and the dungeon filled with rock and dust. In the cave, we hurried to leave for fear that the palace would come down on us. At the cave opening, we decided it would be wise to wait till dawn so we could see better. Ataturk left after telling us to stay. He would be back. We really didn't know if he would be back, but what could we do? At dawn we set out walking.

It was slow going, especially for Anna. We heard horses, so we hid, but when they were in sight, we could see it was Ataturk. Wow, four horses! We didn't ask questions, we just mounted and rode all day, and at dusk we stopped in a little town to eat and rest. Anna was really sick and needed more than just one night, but we were afraid to stop any longer. On the second night, we decided to sleep out in the woods. We built a fire and lay down to rest. As we woke, the sun was just coming up. It was a beautiful sight till we saw Ataturk sitting on a log with a rifle across his lap. "I want all the jewels you have," He said.

"Okay, okay,"

We emptied our pockets and he left, but first he told us never return to the secret room. It was his.

We had no intention of ever coming back to this place. We just wanted to get home with Anna. We were in Greece now, so some of the pressure was off. All the Turkish officials wanted was for us to get out of Turkey. They wanted Ataturk because they couldn't find the treasures of his father. The rest of our journey was uneventful. We took the boat to New York and then the train to Missouri. As we reached New York, you could feel the tension leave us, and as we were speeding to Missouri, each turn of the wheels seemed to be welcoming us back. I can't explain the difference. The old country, for whatever reason, seemed unreal. Why? People fighting each other seemed very unreal. At home, Ann had delivered little Rose. What a homecoming! Rose was all sweet and pink and laughing all the time. I was a lucky man. Four women loved me. The wedding was all arranged, and to our surprise, Anna gave Athena a jeweled necklace. When asked about it, she said, "Long hair hides lots of things!" Of course, everything went off great. I could have sworn I saw Ataturk. It must have been be my imagination. Yet, as I stood beside Athena while waiting to walk down the aisle, I remembered the luxury of traveling as a wealthy person and the rich food and all the lovely things in the palace. How I would love to give my family the things the secret room could provide. Oh well, let her take my arm and walk slowly down the aisle. Who knows what tomorrow will bring? Life gets better and better.

ABOUT THE AUTHOR

As the second child of 14, I grew up fast. There was always so much to do and everyone had a job – children to care for, the house to clean, laundry, etc. I always wanted to read and go to school. That I did when I was in my forties. As I met more and more people, I wanted to know all about them. I always wanted to know more and more including all the details. In 1946, or thereabout, I listened to an elderly man talk about his experience in leaving Armenia. I was fascinated by his story. It haunted me for years. I wanted to write about it, but didn't until now. Could I be the Grandma Moses of literature?

Melva Thorpe
15 Lake Pembroke Dr.
Saint Louis, MO 63135-1210

Printed in the United States
91639LV00006B/3/A

9 781434 319005